Your Treasure Hunt

Disabilities and Finding Your Gold

KATHERINE SCHNEIDER, PhD

ISBN 10: 1-59298-320-0
ISBN 13: 978-1-59298-320-9

Library of Congress Catalog Number: 2009943876

Printed in the United States of America

First Printing: 2010

14 13 12 11 10   5 4 3 2 1

Cover and interior design by James Monroe Design, LLC.

Beaver's Pond Press, Inc.
7104 Ohms Lane, Suite 101
Edina, MN 55439–2129
(952) 829-8818
www.BeaversPondPress.com

To order, visit www.BeaversPondBooks.com
or call (800) 901-3480. Reseller discounts available.

To those who equip our children
for the treasure hunts in life

Thank you!

Dear Parent or Friend of Children,

Thank you for reading this book with a child and for wanting to teach that child about people with disabilities. Aren't children wonderfully curious about differences? You may sometimes feel uncomfortable when your child asks about people with differences and about their own differences. But when you answer a child's question about why a blind person is feeling "those bumps" on an elevator panel, you're giving a strong positive message that it's okay to notice differences, and it's okay to be different. You're also teaching that child how people with disabilities build full lives. I hope this book will help answer some of the other questions your child may ask, like "Tommy makes fun of me and calls me a retard; what can I do?" and "Is it scary to be blind?"

If your child has disabilities, you may be wondering what kind of adult life awaits your child. You want to help them become the resilient, competent, and all-around wonderful human being you know they are.

I grew up blind. I've written this book for you and your child, not to be inspirational, but to help both of you to address the issues that face children with disabilities. I hope that you and your child will enjoy learning about ways to get over, around, or through the barriers on the treasure hunts of life. I also hope this book triggers conversations about important things in life, like hurt feelings and what to do about them, heroes, and the dreams you and your child have for who he or she will become.

This book is a place to start. You, as a parent or caring adult, are on your own treasure hunt. You're learning how to help this child grow up to live a wonderful, full life. You have your own fears and frustrations. For more help on your treasure hunt of raising a child with a disability, contact your local school system or public library for referrals to local support groups, or check out some of the resources listed at the end of the book in the Organizations, Books, and Web Sites section.

Happy treasure hunting!
Katherine Schneider, PhD

Greetings

Have you ever been on a treasure hunt?
Maybe it was a little one, like looking for hidden birthday presents.

This book is about some little treasure hunts,
but it's also about a big treasure hunt:
what kind of a person will you grow up to be?

When you're out looking for treasure, you'll need clues.
Someone might leave you a note. It sure helps if you can read print with your eyes
or Braille with your fingers. Or you can ask someone to read the note to you.
Maybe you'll find a map with all the curb cuts marked.

Everyone's treasure hunt is different, and you never know quite what you'll dig up
or where you'll find it. May I tell you some stories about growing up blind?
Maybe I can give you some clues for your life's treasure hunt.

Come sit down beside Fran.

I was born very early ("premature," as the doctors call it).
My eyes could only see big things and very bright colors.
When I was six months old, my parents took me to several special doctors
to see if my eyes could be fixed. The doctors said they couldn't do anything.

So I went to a preschool class where blind and sighted children learned
and played together. I set off on my life's treasure hunt.

You need to be strong, brave, and smart on your treasure hunt.
Your parents, teachers, and therapists can show you how.

I figured out I was blind when I was three. I was digging up dandelions in the backyard with my older brother, who could see. We got a penny for each dandelion we dug out.
I could see the dandelion's yellow flower only if I was on top of it. My brother was getting to them first because he could see them better.

I was really mad! I lay down on the ground and kicked and screamed. I wanted those pennies so I could buy a doll— a real treasure! But my path was blocked.

Sometimes your path is blocked and you may get mad and sad.

What makes you mad? What makes you sad? What makes you scared?

What can you do instead of kicking and screaming?
Instead of just kicking and screaming you could:

⭐ Talk to a friend. (Here's a clue: some friends have four legs.)

⭐ Toss rocks in a pond or throw snowballs at a tree.

⭐ Listen to music. Dance and sing along.

⭐ Draw a mad picture; then crumple it up and throw it away.

After doing these things, you'll feel better and can go back to your treasure hunt.
I got tired of kicking and screaming, so I went back to digging.
I finally did get enough dandelions dug out of the lawn to buy the doll I wanted.
I was so proud of that doll!

When you're having a tough time, it helps to think about all the things you can do: smile, laugh, cry, ask questions, tell a joke, solve a puzzle, sing a song, make your parents smile, say "Hi" to someone you don't know, listen to a friend.

What else can you do?

In grade school, I went to a special class for an hour a day to learn to read Braille, to type on a typewriter (this was before computers!), and to use a cane for traveling. I hated being different.

If you have a disability, you have learned things that not everyone knows how to do, like how to use a cane if you are blind, how to get around in a wheelchair if you need one, or how to sign and read lips if you are deaf. Learning these things takes extra time and work,

but they make you stronger and smarter.

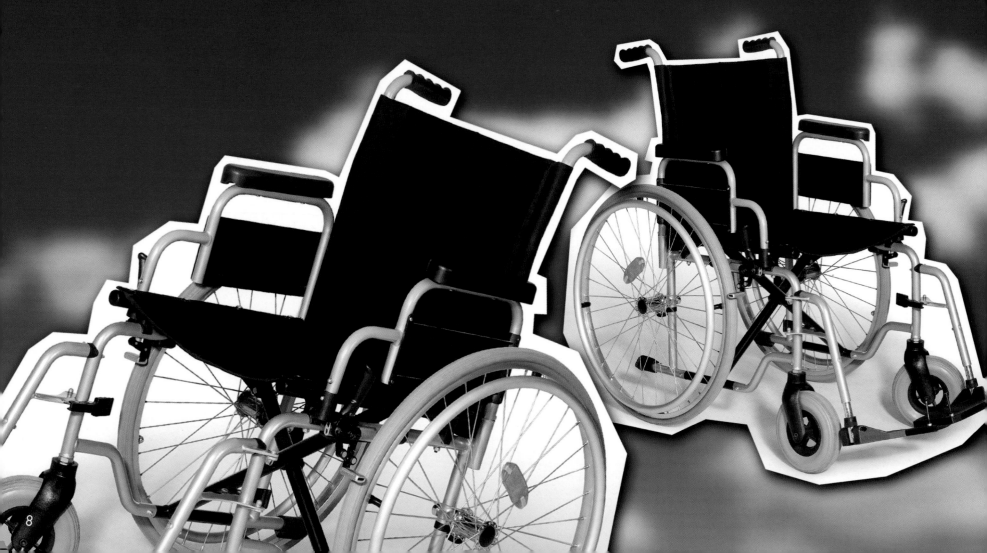

Sometimes it's fun to be different.

When I was your age I could read Braille books in bed at night without turning on the light and getting caught by my parents.

If you have a disability, what is fun about it?
What treasures has your disability brought you?

9

I remember being teased when we read a poem in third grade about seven blind men going to see an elephant. The kids in my class laughed at me because the men in the poem didn't know what an elephant looked like. All I could think to say to them was "shut up!"

Everybody gets teased, but you may get extra teasing because you are different. People may call you "dumb," "retard," "spaz," or other nasty names. Tell them to stop. Turn your back and walk away. Ask your parents or teachers for help if the name-calling continues. Be sure you don't say nasty things to the name-caller. Being mean won't stop someone else from being mean.

What did you do the last time you were teased?

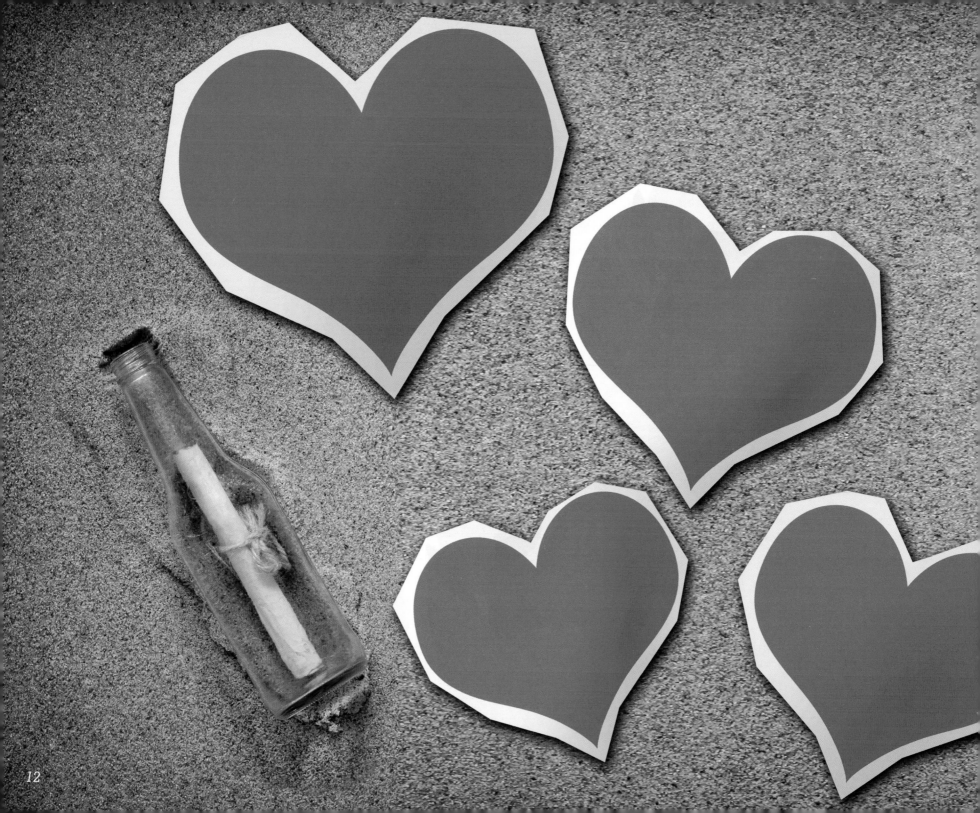

Sometimes it just hurts to be different.

If you're blind and everybody else is laughing at a cartoon you can't see, it hurts. You can ask people to tell you about it, but it isn't the same. Do you feel different sometimes? When?

When it hurts to be different, telling a parent, teacher, or friend can help. These people are treasures. They can listen, give you a hug, and tell you they care. They can't make the hard part about being different go away, but they can share the load.

If nobody is around to help you, give yourself a pep talk in your head. Tell yourself: "Yes I can," "I think I can," "Nobody is perfect," and "I am somebody." This will help to get your heart happy and get you ready to go back to your treasure hunt.

On your treasure hunt you will meet many people. Some will help you, and some you can help.
If they offer to help you by opening the door, and you want the help, say "Yes, please." When you say "Thanks" afterwards,
it makes them feel good. They helped you open the door. You helped them feel good.

Sometimes help isn't helpful. One day I was waiting to cross a busy street.
I was listening carefully for it to be quiet and safe to cross. A big, tall man (he seemed like a giant to me!) came up and,
without saying a word, started to push me across the street.
I said "No!" and didn't move. I wanted to decide when to cross the street.

14

Maybe you don't want help crossing the street. You just want to wait on the corner for your friend.
Say "No, thanks!" loud and clear.

Trying new things is scary for everyone.

But when you have a disability, there are extra challenges.
I remember being scared to go to a book discussion club for teens
at our library because I wouldn't be able to tell where the chairs in the
discussion circle were or which ones were empty.

It was a hassle to ask someone to tap an empty chair so
I could hear where it was. I didn't like being the center of attention.
But I decided the hassle was worth living through to get the treasure
of ideas of new books to read.

What are things that you are scared to do?
How do you decide which ones you will try?

As you grow up, you get to answer
two big questions:

What will I do?

Who will I be?

You may get clues about what you will do when you're grown up.
Look for clues in classes that you're good at, hobbies that you enjoy, and jobs you like to do at home or in school.
Adults have jobs, and so will you someday. Some jobs are paid, like being a firefighter.
I was a college teacher and a counselor who helped students feel better.

Some jobs are volunteer, like being a parent or a friend.
Maybe you could help walk dogs or cuddle cats at the animal shelter.
I was a foster mother for teenagers.
What skills will you need to be a good mother, father, or friend?

You can figure out who you will be by looking inside and asking yourself questions like:

Do I tell the truth?
Do I try to be kind?
Do I say "I'm sorry" when I hurt someone?
Do I say "Thanks" when someone gives me something or helps me?

To help you remember to be kind, honest, and polite, you can think about a hero you have who is kind and polite.
Who are your heroes? These can be people you know, or they can be famous people.

When I was in fifth grade, I decided I wanted to be a scientist. My parents took me to meet a blind math teacher. I wanted to be just like him—I even wanted a parakeet like the one he had.

Do you have a hero who has a disability? If you don't, ask your teacher, school counselor, or librarian to help you find some heroes with disabilities. You might find heroes who are real people, or heroes who are characters in books or movies.

—searching for who you will be and what you will do—goes on forever. You'll get bigger, smarter, and stronger, but you'll always find new treasures.

I'm a grown-up, and I'm still finding treasures!
This year, I found a pineapple banana cake recipe using
my talking computer and the Internet.
Then I changed it to make it more heart-healthy.

I've also enjoyed learning to do Sudoku puzzles
with Brailled numbers.

Puzzles make you think. I feel so happy
when I figure them out. Do you like puzzles?

Just imagine what you'll find on your life's treasure hunt.

Have a great treasure hunt and a great life!

Organizations, Books, & Resources

Books for Adults

Brodey, Denise. *The Elephant in the Playroom: Ordinary Parents Write Intimately and Honestly About the Extraordinary Highs and Heartbreaking Lows of Raising Kids with Special Needs.* New York: Hudson Street Press, 2007.

Fawcett, Heather, and Amy Baskin. *More than a Mom: Living a Full and Balanced Life When Your Child has Special Needs.* Bethesda, MD: Woodbine House Special Needs Books, 2006.

Gill, Barbara. *Changed by a Child: Companion Notes for Parents of a Child with a Disability.* Warner, NH: Mainstreet Books, 1998.

Klein, Stanley D., and Kim Schive, eds. *You Will Dream New Dreams: Inspiring Personal Stories by Parents of Children With Disabilities.* New York: Kensington Publishing Corp., 2001.

Klein, Stanley D. and John D. Kemp, eds. Foreword by Marlee Matlin. *Reflections From a Different Journey: What Adults With Disabilities Wish All Parents Knew.* Imprint New York : McGraw-Hill, 2004.

Marshak, Laura E., and Fran P. Prezant. *Married with Special Needs Children: A Couples' Guide to Keeping Connected.* Bethesda, MD: Woodbine House Special Needs Books, 2007.

Children's Books

Winners of the American Library Association's Schneider Family Book Awards:

Abeel, Samantha. (2003). *My Thirteenth Winter.*

Bertrand Gonzales, Diane (2004). *My Pal Victor.*

Clements, Andrew. (2002). *Things Not Seen.*

Connor, Leslie. (2008) *Waiting For Normal.*

Friesen, Jonathan. (2008) *Jerk, California.*

Fusco, Kimberly Newton. (2004). *Tending to Grace.*

Lang, Glenna. (2003). *Looking Out for Sarah.*

Lord, Cynthia. (2006). *Rules.*

Mass, Wendy. (2003). *A Mango-Shaped Space.*

Parker, Robert A. (2008) *Piano Starts Here: The Young Art Tatum.*

Rapp, Adam. (2004). *Under the Wolf, Under the Dog.*

Rorby, Ginny. (2006). *Hurt Go Happy.*

Ryan, Pam Munoz. (2004). *Becoming Naomi Leon.*

Sachar, Louis. (2006). *Small Steps.*

Seeger, Pete, and Paul DuBois Jacobs. (2006). *The Deaf Musicians.*

Stryer, Andrea Stenn. (2006). *Kami and the Yaks.*

Uhlberg, Myron. (2004). *Dad, Jackie, and Me.*

Zimmer, Tracie Vaughn. (2007). *Reaching for Sun.*

Sources of Books in Alternate Format

American Printing House for the Blind
(502) 895-2405
www.aph.org

Bookshare
www.bookshare.org

National Library Service for the Blind and Physically Handicapped
(NLS)
www.loc.gov/nls
Contact NLS for your state library's information.

Recording for the Blind and Dyslexic (RFB&D)
(609) 452-0606
(800) 221-4972 (book orders only)
www.rfbd.org

Organizations and Web Sites

American Council of the Blind (ACB)/Council of Families
with Visual Impairments
(800) 424-8666
www.acb.org

American Foundation for the Blind (AFB)
(800) 232-5463
www.afb.org

The Arc
www.thearc.org

Children's Disabilities Information
http://www.childrensdisabilities.info/adhd/index.html

Disability Resources on the Internet
http://www.disabilityresources.org/

EP Global Communications, Inc.
http://www.eparent.com/

Family Village
http://www.familyvillage.wisc.edu/

Hadley School for the Blind
www.hadley.edu

National Association for Parents of the Visually Impaired
(800) 562-6265
www.spedex.com/napvi

National Association of the Deaf
http://www.nad.org/

National Federation of the Blind (NFB)
(410) 659-9314
www.nfb.org

Pacer Center
http://www.pacer.org/pandr/

Parenting Special-Needs Magazine
http://parentingspecialneeds.org/

Special Child
http://www.specialchild.com/index.html

United Cerebral Palsy
http://www.ucp.org/

U.S. Department of Education Disability Resources Website
http://www.ed.gov/parents/needs/speced/edpicks.jhtml

Acknowledgements

In writing and publishing this book, I've encountered a number of human treasures and one canine treasure I'd like to thank.

- The Foundations of Education and Editing classes at the University of Wisconsin–Eau Claire, whose faculty and students have generously shared their reactions to the book.

- Ruth Cronje, for her excellent initial edits and encouragement to go forth and find a publisher.

- The professionals at Beaver's Pond Press, who are good at their jobs and humane to amateur authors.

- Kellie Hultgren, who was willing to try editing over the phone with me.

- Jay Monroe, for rising to the challenge of designing graphics to achieve my vision for the book.

- Maradeth Searle, friend, colleague and eyes during the graphic design stage of publishing this book.

- Marge Bottoms, photographer extraordinaire for portraits of Fran and me.

- Fran, my Seeing-Eye dog, who walked and sat beside me throughout the writing, editing, and publishing process.